Aardman
Presents

Wallace & Gromit ™
CARAVAN OF TERROR

WRITTEN BY GLENN DAKIN
ILLUSTRATED BY STUART TROTTER

POCKET
BOOKS

"I've got a surprise for you, Gromit old lad!" declared Wallace over tea and toast one morning.

Gromit peered right and left. He looked up at the ceiling and under the table. Surprises from Wallace usually came out of a cannon at 100 miles an hour. But this time there was nothing, just Wallace beaming at him with a toothy grin.

VISIT BLEAKLY-ON-SEA

"My Uncle Eric has a caravan at Bleakly-on-Sea, and he's written to say we can stay there for a week!"

He slapped a brochure down on the table showing a pretty caravan park overlooking a long golden beach and a blue sea twinkling in the sunshine. There was even a palm tree invitingly framing the scene.
"We're going on holiday!" Wallace grinned.

THE NORTH WEST'S COSTA DEL SOL

Sheets of icy rain swept across the cliff as Wallace brought the motorbike to a halt at the Bleakly-on-Sea caravan park. Rain dripped off the wooden leaves of the fake palm tree that stood at the gate. A grey sea rumbled in the distance.

"Here we are, Gromit!" Wallace beamed. "Bracing, isn't it?"
Waiting for them at the entrance was a wizened, sad-looking man.

"I'm Mr Tweezers," said the man. "Caretaker of the caravan park. And please remember, you're not here to go mad. We don't like merrymakers in these parts. Keep the noise down, don't make a mess and keep that dangerous-looking dog of yours under control."

"Gromit isn't dangerous," replied Wallace. "He's got a first aid certificate from St John's Ambulance."

That evening, the rain stopped and Gromit set up a picnic table outside the caravan. Their meal was interrupted when a great white bird landed slap-bang in the middle of the salt and pepper, letting out an ear-piercing cry.

"He wants your chips, Gromit!" chortled Wallace. Wallace offered Gromit's plate to the bird, but it screeched again and flapped its wings so wildly the chips flew everywhere.

"He's a bit big for a seagull, isn't he Gromit?" Wallace said. They had both fled to the safety of the van, their noses pressed up against the window.

The bird shrieked for a final time then flew away into the dusk. "Well, I never!" said Wallace. "I reckon that was an albatross. If you see one it means very good luck!" Then he pondered for a moment. "Or does it mean complete and utter disaster? Hmm…"

While Wallace and Gromit slept that night, Mr Tweezers cleared away the scattered chips. "Holiday-makers!" he grumbled. "This site would be better off without them…"

The next morning, Wallace
bounded down the caravan
steps in his best holiday clothes.
Gromit, already waiting outside,
paled. It was a sight not easily
forgotten.

"Who's for the beach?" Wallace grinned.
"The beach? That's for cissies, that is!" boomed a great voice nearby.
They turned to see a beefy man in long socks and hiking boots.

"I'm off for a hike up Madman's Ridge. Beamish is the name. Bob Beamish when I'm on holiday, Robert when I'm not." He shook hands with Wallace.

"Lovely place isn't it?" Wallace said. "Grand view."

Bob Beamish frowned. "It would be if I could see it," he growled. "But your blinking caravan is right in the way of my view. I can't see a thing."

"Oh dear," said Wallace. "Well, enjoy Madman's Ridge!"

Bob strode off. "At least up there I won't have to look at your blimmin' caravan!" he shouted back.

"You're lucky, Gromit," Wallace said, as they arrived at the beach. "Carrying all those boxes on your head is protecting you from this headwind. There's certainly a nip in the air."

Gromit plodded on, feeling like an arctic explorer, not a holiday-maker.

Wallace chose a spot, then grabbed a contraption from under Gromit's arm.

"My self-erecting windbreak!" he grinned, pressing a button on the side. In a whirlwind of wooden poles and stripy cloth it sprang to life and unfolded itself. Unfortunately, Gromit was standing a little too close and it catapulted him ears over tail into a rock pool.

Gromit emerged from the water draped in seaweed, to see Wallace lying back in his deckchair, protected by his windbreak, covered by a big colourful umbrella and drinking hot tea from a flask.

"Ho ho, very good, Gromit – you look like the Loch Ness Monster!" Wallace smiled. "I must take a picture!"

Doggedly determined to enjoy himself, Gromit set to work on a rather nice little sandcastle. He tipped up his bucket, and the sand came out in a perfect little hill.

"You needn't tire yourself out, lad!" Wallace shouted. "Look, I've invented a bucket-and-spade-omatic!" Out of a box came Wallace's new sandcastle-making machine.

At the press of a button it chugged noisily to life. Sand was sucked up one end, analysed (so that shells, pebbles and crabs could be sifted out), then squirted into a series of revolving buckets. Meanwhile, robotic hands built battlements, dug moats, made towers and even popped little flags into them.

But Wallace's delight in his new invention was cut short. Suddenly the machine swung round and started to build sandcastles on top of him.
"Help!" he cried. "Gromit – I think some sand must have got in the works!"

Gromit tried desperately to stop the machine, but it kept building walls and moats to prevent him reaching its 'off' switch. At one point it had Gromit ringed in three walls of pebble-dashed battlements, but he managed to tunnel out.

"Attaboy, Gromit!" Wallace cried encouragingly.

Gromit finally cornered the bucket-and-spade-omatic by the sewage outflow and switched it off with a broken badminton racket that had been washed up in a storm.

Gromit turned to find Wallace, and saw that the entire beach was now one big sandcastle. But it was nice and peaceful in a funny sort of way, with Wallace in the distance, buried under the sand.

When Gromit finally got back, Wallace sighed with relief. "I don't know how you stopped that machine, Gromit, but well done." Then he eyed Gromit in a puzzled way. "And by the way, this is NO time for badminton."

They arrived back at their van to an extraordinary spectacle. A skull and crossbones made of shells and pebbles lay outside their door. It had a decided air of menace.

"Ooh dear!" cooed Wallace. "Is someone trying to frighten us?"
Mr Tweezers walked by. "Enjoyed making that did you?" he snapped.
"But… but… but!" sputtered Wallace.

Tweezers loomed over him. "Of course, muggins here has to clear it up!" he grumbled, pointing to himself. "And I'll have to tidy all that grass again," he muttered. "I only straightened it all out this morning. Each blade eight millimetres apart for best effect, according to tourist council guidelines. Not that you'd appreciate that. Hooligans! I'll be late for my other job now," he added angrily.

Wallace rubbed his head. "Well, here's a how-do-you-do!" he said.

They retired to their caravan. Gromit frowned as a fresh squall of icy rain lashed against the window.

"Never mind old lad!" smiled Wallace. "I've brought my All-purpose, Auto-assembling, Rainy-day Games Compendium with built in Robo-Ref in case of any… ahem, cheating!"

In moments the rainy day was forgotten – except by Gromit who had to nip outside and fix the electricity generator which Wallace's device was overloading every ten minutes.

At lunch-time the clouds parted and they decided to take the air down at the seafront. Wallace's eyes lit up when he saw a winkle stall.

"Well well, so you run this too!" smiled Wallace. Mr Tweezers snorted.

"Yes, and I was lucky I opened at all today, thanks to you!"

"I do like the look of your pickled whelks," said Wallace, placatingly.

"Come round the back…" Mr Tweezers replied, "and you'll find out that whelks aren't the only things I pickle…"

As Wallace stepped inside, Mr Tweezers picked up a heavy object…

"Ooh yes, roll mops and winkles!" Wallace said when he saw the goodies inside. Suddenly, a shadow fell across him, and he whirled around. There was Mr Tweezers holding up the biggest piece of novelty rock Wallace had ever seen.

"And I sell these too!" said Mr Tweezers. "It says 'Bleakly-on-Sea' all the way through!"

"Cracking!" said Wallace. "I'll take two!"

Wallace and Gromit gnawed their rock on a windswept bench, watching the drizzle blow across the empty strand.

"Grand holiday, eh pooch?" Wallace remarked. Gromit said nothing. Then Wallace spotted a sign that said: 'Punch and Judy, two o'clock at the pier.' "Champion!" Wallace said. "That sounds like fun, Gromit!"

They strolled up to the pier at two, but there was nobody to be seen at the Punch and Judy Show. In fact, a grisly scene had just taken place on the miniature stage. The baby was lying in the crocodile's mouth and Mr Punch was tied up in a string of sausages.

In the distance, Gromit pointed at the fleeing figure of the Punch and Judy Man, who was shouting wildly. Wallace listened hard.

"I'm not sure," Wallace frowned, "but I think he said his name was Albert Ross…"

That afternoon they went to the putting green, but somebody had pulled out all the flags. Wallace couldn't even have a go on the one-armed bandit, because the coin slot had been jammed with seaweed. Gloomily, they walked back to the caravan site. "It almost seems as if somebody is trying to ruin our holiday!" Wallace said.

When they got back to the caravan park, there was another shock. The window of their caravan was wide open. "Oh dear, I hope nothing's been taken!" worried Wallace.

But when they looked inside, it was soon clear that nothing was missing. Wallace decided to go to bed early. "There Gromit, nothing to worry about at all!" he beamed. "Isn't it silly how your imagination can run riot!" He picked up his mug of cocoa and pulled back his blanket...

Wallace leapt out of his skin — his bed was a seething, wriggling heap of crabs, eels and slimy jellyfish. Wallace was shaking all over. "Gromit!" he cried.

A bloodcurdling screech filled the air, and Wallace saw the eye of the albatross staring in at the window. A tell-tale frond of seaweed in his beak showed that he had been responsible.

"YOU!" Wallace shouted. "Come on Gromit — I've had enough. We're getting out of here!"

Wallace and Gromit raced out — but just as they were fleeing through the door, Wallace slipped on a jellyfish and crashed to the floor. Gromit turned back to help him when suddenly there was a terrifying, cataclysmic rumbling…

Before Gromit's horrified eyes, a huge crack split the ground. The cliff shuddered and an avalanche of rock tumbled away into the sea. The caravan, with Wallace inside it, slid towards the edge of a sheer drop.

Gromit was suddenly aware that the albatross was next to him. It pointed a wing at the scene of disaster and gave him a meaningful and not unkindly look.

In a flash, Gromit realised that the albatross had known all along that the cliff was dangerous. It had been trying to drive them out for their own safety!

There was another deafening rumble. The cliff shook again, and the caravan slid further over the edge. The caravan door flapped open as Wallace slid towards the back of the van. Wallace was wobbling on the brink of destruction!

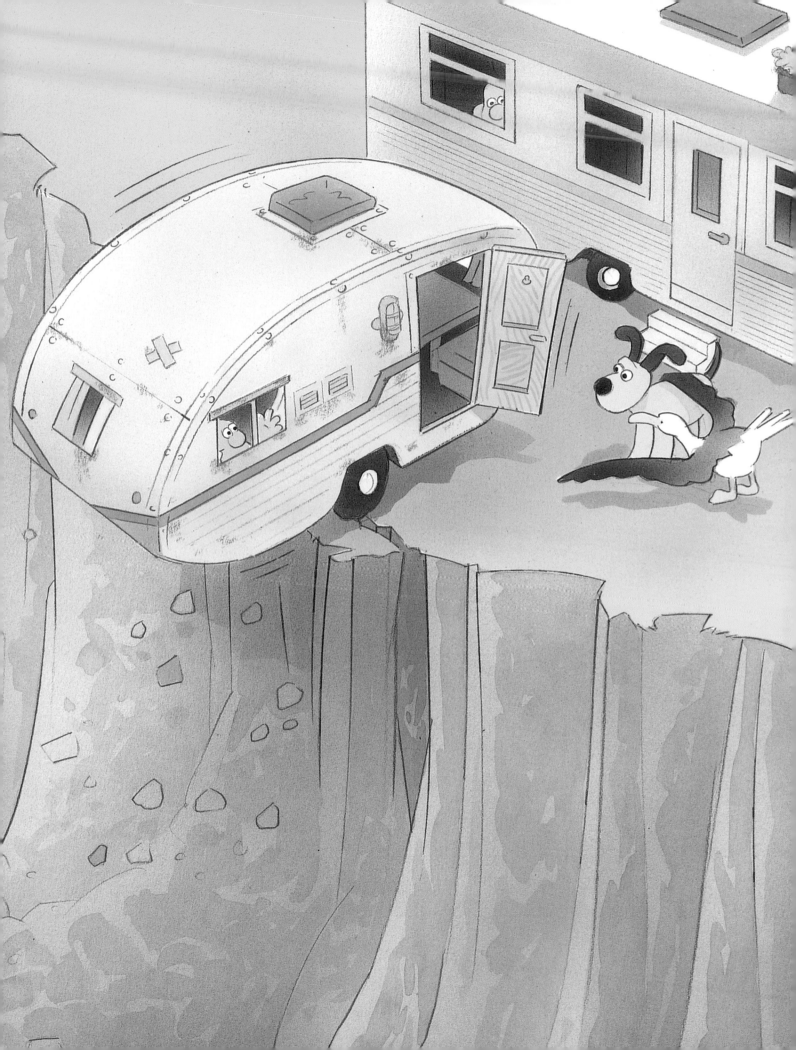

"Gromit!" Wallace wailed. "Save me!"

Through the van door, Gromit spotted a red button peeping out of the debris. He turned to the albatross, and pointed at the button. They exchanged a nod.
"Helllllp!" Wallace cried.
The albatross swooped into the van.

It pecked at the button and suddenly Wallace's self erecting windbreak burst into life. There was a click, a whir, a flurry of poles, and Wallace was hurled out of the door with a great *poinnng!*

Wallace flew to safety just as the caravan tumbled over the cliff.

"What happened?" asked Bob Beamish, emerging from the shower block in a towel. Wallace rubbed his head.

"Well we thought someone wanted to drive us away and spoil our holiday – but in fact this albatross was trying to save us all along. It must have known that the cliff was going to collapse. It can't talk, of course, so it tried to make us leave any way it could. Albatrosses are very deep, you know. They have a reputation for being birds of fateful omen."

"Fantastic!" said Bob.

"It is quite a tale," Wallace agreed.

"No, I mean it's fantastic for me," Bob replied. "Now that your caravan has gone, I have the best view in the park!"

Mr Tweezers appeared behind them in his usual mysterious way. "You've been very careless with that van of yours," he said sadly. "I always knew you were a right pair."

"I hope you don't mind," Wallace said to Gromit the next day, "that we've had to spend the rest of our holiday at a guest house." His eyes lit up as the landlady set a great dish of eggs and bacon in front of him. "Normally," Wallace explained to his hostess, "Gromit likes to cook for me – and wash up, of course!"

Gromit didn't mind one bit. As he fed a morsel of buttered kipper to the albatross on the window sill, he felt that he was really on holiday at last.